WE ARE NOT
FROGS!

WE ARE NOT FROGS!

MICHAEL MORPURGO

With illustrations by
Sam Usher

Barrington Stoke

First published in 2018 in Great Britain by
Barrington Stoke Ltd
18 Walker Street, Edinburgh, EH3 7LP

www.barringtonstoke.co.uk

This Little Gem edition based on
We Are Not Frogs! (Barrington Stoke, 2016)

This story was first published in a different form in
Animal Stories for the Very Young (Kingfisher, 1994)

Text © 1994 & 2018 Michael Morpurgo
Illustrations © 2016 Sam Usher

A CIP catalogue record for this book is available
from the British Library upon request

ISBN: 978-1-78112-792-6

Printed in China by Leo

This book is in a super readable format for young readers
beginning their independent reading journey.

For Sylvie and Oscar,
and their mum and dad too

CONTENTS

CHAPTER 1

A SHAGGY DOG STORY

The storm was over and all the frogs and
toads came hopping out onto the lawn
to play long-jump. The frogs always
chose long-jump because frogs can jump
further than toads. And, of course, the
frogs always won. The toads didn't
mind all that much.

'Anything for a quiet life,' the toads thought.

All of a sudden, the door of the house opened. Mutt, a shaggy sort of sheepdog, came bounding out to bark at a lorry that was coming up the road.

The frogs scattered into the safety of the flowerbeds under the porch and hid. The toads could not move so fast. So, instead, they stayed very still where they were and just hoped they would not be trodden on, nor eaten.

They were in luck. Mutt went roaring after the lorry, chasing it all the way along the fence until he was quite sure it would never come back. Then, with his tail high, and wagging with pride, he walked over to the porch and lay down in the shade. Soon he was fast asleep, his head on his paws.

CHAPTER 2

A QUIET LIFE

It wasn't long after this that two children came wandering out onto the lawn. Jago was pulling a small cart. Alice was sitting inside the cart, and both of them were reading.

They were taking turns pulling, but it always seemed to be Jago's turn.

'Anything for a quiet life,' he thought.

The toads were sitting in the long grass and did not see them coming till it was too late. There was only time to shout.

"Watch out! Watch out!" the chief toad croaked.

He was the chief because he was the
biggest and he had the loudest voice.

But Jago and Alice heard nothing.

They were far too busy reading.

It was very lucky for the toads that Alice finished her book just at that moment. She looked up and saw them.

"Look," she said. "Frogs!"

"We're NOT frogs," the chief toad croaked. He was quite annoyed, but no one heard him.

CHAPTER 3

TOADS DON'T JUMP

Alice and Jago kneeled down in the grass and caught the toads one by one in cupped hands with great care, and put them in an ice-cream carton. Soon there were so many of them that they were all clambering on top of each other to get out.

"That's the lot," Alice cried, and she clapped her hands in glee. "We've got 14 frogs. Perfect."

"We're NOT frogs," the chief toad croaked, but the two children were now too busy talking to hear him.

"They're all warty," Jago said, "and they feel dry and bumpy." And he poked one to make it jump. It didn't, so he tried another. "And they don't jump."

"All frogs jump," Alice said, and she peered into the carton.

Now the chief toad was really angry, and he croaked louder than he'd ever croaked before, at the top of his croaky voice. This time they heard him. This time they had to listen.

"How many times do I have to tell you that we're NOT frogs?" he croaked. "And will you please stop poking us? We are toads, and toads don't jump – not if we can help it anyway."

"Well," Alice said, "frogs aren't much fun if they don't jump."

CHAPTER 4

A MUDDY DITCH

The chief toad thought as fast as he
could. "I tell you what," he said. "You
put us all back – with great care, mind –
in our nice muddy ditch at the bottom
of the garden, and I'll tell you where
you can find real proper frogs that jump
much much better than we ever could."

The children agreed right away and
carried the toads down the garden to

their muddy ditch where they emptied
them out, but carefully, very carefully.

"Thank you kindly," the chief toad croaked. "To tell you the truth, we wouldn't have been very happy in your house. We like it muddy, you see – all toads do."

"What about the frogs?" Alice said. She had no patience. "These jumping frogs. Where are they?"

"Over there," the chief toad croaked. "In the flowerbed by the steps. You can't miss them. They'll be jumping." And with a toady smile he sank into the mud and was gone.

CHAPTER 5

JUMP LIKE
A KANGAROO

Of course, the children found the frogs right where the chief toad had told them. There were 22 of them. Alice counted them, and that was hard because they kept jumping all over the place.

Catching them wasn't easy either,
but at last they were all safe and sound
in the carton, where they jumped
up and down trying to get out.

"Good jumpers, these," Jago said.

"That's because they're frogs," said
Alice. "But if they were kangaroos,
they'd be even jumpier. I wish they were
kangaroos!"

And just then Granny called out of the window. "Tea time. Chocolate cake!"

"Chocolate cake!" they cried. "Whoopee! Yummy, yum, yum!"

And they left behind the carton with the 22 frogs, and ran.

The frogs jumped and jumped, but the sides were too high and they just couldn't jump out, no matter how hard they tried.

CHAPTER 6

IT'S A DOG'S LIFE

Back on the porch, Mutt began to wake from a dream in which he was burying the bones of a very large lorry. A wasp walked along his nose and buzzed, so he woke up faster.

He shook the wasp off and stood up and stretched and yawned.

As he lifted his nose he smelled something he liked. It smelled to him a lot like chocolate cake.

He licked his lips and padded across
the lawn towards the kitchen.

Mutt was just passing the cart when
he saw the carton – or rather he heard
it.

He looked inside. 'Jumping frogs,' he thought. 'Interesting.'

He sniffed at the frogs and they jumped up at his nose.

So Mutt barked at them and then tried to touch them with his paw, but he knocked over the carton instead.

The frogs spilled out over the lawn. Away they went, jumping across the long grass in 22 different directions. Mutt could not make up his mind which one to chase, and so in the end he chased none of them.

He was cross with himself, and so he chased the carton all over the lawn instead and pounced on it and chewed it and shook it.

By then Mutt was very pleased with himself.

So he carried the carton into the kitchen to show everyone.

CHAPTER 7

AFTER THE STORM

The moment the children saw the empty carton they burst into tears.

"Our frogs," they said. "Mutt's gone and eaten our jumping frogs!"

"They were our frogs," Alice cried. "We had 22 and now he's eaten them all."

"I won't ever talk to Mutt again," said Jago, and he pulled the carton out of Mutt's mouth and pushed him into his basket.

"Me too," said Alice. "We'll none of us ever speak to him again."

And they both cried a lot more, and loudly too.

But Granny was looking out of the window. "I think you'd better come and see," she said, and she pointed. "Over there by the flowerbed."

And when they looked they saw 22 happy frogs hopping away, all perfectly alive and uneaten.

Can you count all 22 frogs?

"Well," said Granny. "Shall we have our chocolate cake now? And I think poor Mutt deserves a treat too, don't you? He doesn't look at all happy. Let's cheer him up, shall we?"

So they tickled Mutt to cheer him up and gave him a dog chew. Then they sat down together for their chocolate cake.

And the children smiled through the last of their tears, just like the summer sun coming out after the storm is over.

Our books are tested
for children and young people by
children and young people.

Thanks to everyone who consulted on
a manuscript for their time and effort in
helping us to make our books better
for our readers.